W9-AQR-177

09/2021

PALM BEACH COUNTY
LIBRARY SYSTEM
3650 Summit Boulevard
West Palm Beach, FL   33406-4198

Star of the Class Play

Written by Margaret McNamara
Illustrated by Mike Gordon

Ready-to-Read

Simon Spotlight

New York   London   Toronto   Sydney   New Delhi

SIMON SPOTLIGHT
An imprint of Simon & Schuster Children's Publishing Division
1230 Avenue of the Americas, New York, New York 10020
This Simon Spotlight edition June 2021
Text copyright © 2021 by Margaret McNamara
Illustrations copyright © 2021 by Mike Gordon
For information about special discounts for bulk purchases, please contact Simon &
Schuster Special Sales at 1-866-506-1949 or business@simonandschuster.com.
Manufactured in the United States of America 0521 LAK
2 4 6 8 10 9 7 5 3 1
Cataloging-in-Publication Data is available for this title from the Library of Congress.
ISBN 978-1-5344-6831-3 (hc)
ISBN 978-1-5344-6830-6 (pbk)
ISBN 978-1-5344-6832-0 (eBook)

"The class play is on Friday,"
said Nia. "I am the star!"
"You will all be stars,"
said Mrs. Connor.

At home Nia practiced.
She put out her arms.
"Welcome to the class play!"
she said loudly.

Her mama clapped.
"I will do it again
even better," said Nia.

She did it again, and again,
and again.

"Now I am ready," Nia said.

Class Play Day came.

Everybody had a costume
and make-up!

The gym was full.

People were smiling,
and waving,
and taking pictures.

"It is time for the play
to start, Nia,"
said Mrs. Connor.

Nia took one step
on the stage.

Her hands shook.
Her legs shook.

Her mouth felt like
a cotton ball.

"I cannot do this!" said Nia.
She ran off the stage.

Mrs. Connor looked right
at Nia.

"I think you can do this,"
Mrs. Connor said.

"You do?" asked Nia.

"Yes," said Mrs. Connor.

"Take three big breaths,"
said Mrs. Connor.

"Count to four as you breathe in," she said. "Count to seven as you breathe out."

Nia breathed in and out
very slowly,
three times in a row.

She felt better!

"Everybody is rooting
for you,"
said Mrs. Connor.
"They are?" asked Nia.

"Yes," said Mrs. Connor.
"Then I will try again,"
said Nia.

Nia went out on stage.

She put out her arms.

"Welcome to the class play!" she said.

Everybody cheered.

When the play was over,
Nia got a hug from her
mama.
"You were the star!"
said her mama.

"We were all stars," said Nia.